This book belongs to:

_____

_____

Berryland Books

Edited by Claire Black
Illustrated by Eric Kincaid

Published by Berryland Books
www.berrylandbooks.com

First published in 2004
Copyright © Berryland Books 2004

ISBN 1-84577-074-9
Printed in China

Puss in Boots

Reading should always be FUN !

Reading is one of the most important skills your child will learn. It's an exciting challenge that you can enjoy together.

Treasured Tales is a collection of stories that has been carefully written for young readers.

Here are some useful points to help you teach your child to read.

Try to set aside a regular quiet time for reading at least three times a week.

Choose a time of the day when your child is not too tired.

Plan to spend approximately 15 minutes on each session.

Select the book together and spend the first few minutes talking about the title and cover picture.

Spend the next ten minutes listening and encouraging your child to read.

Always allow your child to look at and use the pictures to help them with the story.

Spend the last couple of minutes asking your child about what they have read. You will find a few examples of questions at the bottom of some pages.

Understanding what they have read is as important as the reading itself.

There was once a poor miller who died, leaving all he had to his three sons.

The eldest son was given the mill.

The second son was given a donkey.

All that was left for the youngest son was a cat called Puss!

"It's fine for my brothers, they will not starve, but what use is Puss?" he said to himself.

"Even if I skin him and eat him, I will soon be hungry again," he said.

Puss did not like the sound of that and decided to say something.

"Do not despair, my master, I have a plan," he said.

"Fetch me a pair of boots, a hat and a sack."

What did Puss ask his master to fetch?

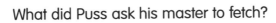

The miller's son was so shocked that Puss could speak, he did as he was told.

Puss put on the boots, the hat and then threw the sack over his shoulder.

He turned around and went into the woods to hunt.

Soon he returned with a large rabbit in the sack.

Instead of eating the rabbit, Puss went to the palace and asked to see the King.

"I have a gift for the King from my master, the Marquis of Carabas," he told the guard.

As Puss was brought before the King, he bowed and opened the sack.

"Your Majesty," he said, "please accept this fine rabbit as a gift from my master, the Marquis of Carabas."

The King was delighted.

"Please thank your master, it is very generous of him," he said.

What did Puss give to the King?

The next day Puss returned to the palace with two plump pheasants.

Once again the King was very happy and asked Puss to give his thanks to the Marquis.

Every day, for several weeks, Puss continued to bring gifts that he said were from his master.

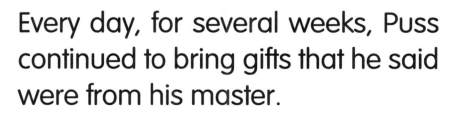

Then one day, he heard that the King and his daughter were going to be traveling through the countryside.

Puss thought of a clever plan.

He ran home and called out to his master, "Take off your clothes and jump into the river!"

His master was surprised but did as Puss asked.

Just then they saw the King's carriage approaching.

Puss shouted "Help! Help! My master, the Marquis of Carabas, is drowning!"

The King looked out and asked the driver to stop.

Puss explained that his master had been robbed of his clothes and thrown into the river.

What did Puss shout out?

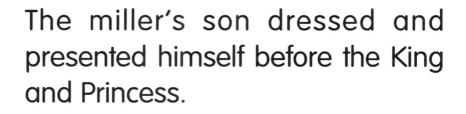

At once the King sent for a set of his finest clothes.

The miller's son dressed and presented himself before the King and Princess.

The King was very impressed and invited him to join them on their journey.

The Princess had fallen in love with the miller's son.

Meanwhile, Puss ran ahead to continue with his plan.

Soon he passed some farmers and told them to say that they were working on land that belonged to the Marquis of Carabas.

As the King approached he asked the farmers whose land they were on.

"We are working on the lands of the Marquis of Carabas," they said and the King was impressed.

What did the King ask the farmers?

Puss continued on until he reached a grand castle.

The castle belonged to an ogre who claimed to have magical powers.

Puss walked in and demanded to see the ogre at once.

"I have heard about your magical powers and traveled far to see for myself," Puss said to the ogre.

"I have heard that you can change yourself into any animal you wish," he continued.

"What you have heard is true," roared the ogre as he turned himself into a lion.

Puss was really afraid but kept quite still.

"Very clever," he said, "but can you turn yourself into something as tiny as a mouse?"

Instantly the ogre changed into a tiny mouse.

What has the ogre changed into now?

Puss did not waste any time.

He pounced on the mouse and gobbled it up.

"Mmmm," said Puss, licking his lips.

Puss then asked the cooks to prepare a wonderful feast.

Next, he went outside to the palace gates and waited for the King.

"Your Majesty," said Puss.

"You are most welcome to the castle of my master, the Marquis of Carabas."

The King, Princess and the Marquis then followed Puss into the castle and sat down to enjoy the food.

Who greeted the King?

The miller's son was amazed at how clever his cat was.

The King was very pleased that his daughter had fallen in love with such a handsome and wealthy man.

When the Marquis asked to marry the Princess, the King happily agreed.

The Princess and Marquis were married soon after.

Puss put away his boots and hat, gave up hunting and lived comfortably ever after.